JUICY
CUT

by

Neena Beber

SAMUEL FRENCH

FOUNDED 1830

New York Hollywood London Toronto

SAMUELFRENCH.COM

IMPORTANT BILLING AND CREDIT REQUIREMENTS

All producers of JUMP/CUT *must* give credit to the Author of the Play in all programs distributed in connection with performances of the Play and in all instances in which the title of the Play appears for purposes of advertising, publicizing or otherwise exploiting the Play and/or a production. The name of the Author *must* appear on a separate line on which no other name appears, immediately following the title, and *must* appear in size of type not less than fifty percent the size of the title type.

In addition, the following credit *must* appear in all programs distributed in connection with the Work:

The New York Premiere of JUMP/CUT
was produced in 2006 by
The Woman's Project
Loretta Greco, Producing Artistic Director   Julie Crosby, Managing Director

Winner of the L. Arnold Weissberger Award 2000

THEATER J AND WOOLLY MAMMOTH THEATRE COMPANY

present

a new play by Neena Beber
directed by Leigh Silverman

Cast
Paul...Eric Sutton*
Dave...Michael Chernus*
Karen...Colleen Delany*

Set Design...Erhard Rom
Lighting Design...Dan Conway
Sound Design...Jill B.C. Du Boff
Costume Design.. Michele Reisch
Properties... Linda S. Evans, Jennifer Peterson
Dramaturg...Mary Resing
Production Stage Manager...Shannon Marie Mayonado*

*Member, Actors' Equity Association

There will be one 15-minute intermission.

**Theater J & Woolly Mammoth would like to thank the following
sponsors for their generous support of *JUMP/CUT*:**

Susan & Dixon Butler
Kenneth W. Crow
Mimi Cutler & Paul Salditt

Catherine MacNeil Hollinger
& Mark Hollinger
The Jacob and Charlotte
Lehrman Foundation
Laura & Gerald Rosberg

Karen & Milton
Schneiderman
Joan S. Wessel
Leslie Westreich

**Woolly Mammoth gratefully acknowledges the generous support of
the following sponsors of its 2002-2003 Season:**

Anne & Ronald Abramson
American Airlines

Pete Miller & Sara Cormeny

Shugoll Research
Washington Plaza Hotel

Jump/Cut was developed through a partnership between Woolly Mammoth
and A.S.K. Theater Projects *New Plays/New Ways* program.

Jump/Cut was also developed through a workshop production at The Gloucester Stage Company
in Massachusetts, Israel Horovitz, Artistic Director, and a developmental workshop at
New Dramatists in New York, Todd London, Artistic Director.

I have sat and listened to too many
words of the collaborating muse,
and plotted perhaps too freely with my life,
not avoiding injury to others,
not avoiding injury to myself--
to ask compassion....

—Robert Lowell, "Dolphin"

CHARACTERS

Paul

Dave

Karen

AUTHOR'S NOTE

Paul's speeches in bold, marked with the stage direction "out," are meant to indicate Paul's present time, direct address to the audience as he presents the story to us. When Dave or Karen's speeches are similarly market, these should be considered as direct to-camera monologues. It is not the playwright's intention to use actual film—rather, a purely theatrical interpretation of the cinematic close-up should be found. In the production directed by Leigh Silverman at Woolly Mammoth/Theatre J, strobe lighting and a film projector sound effect were used to differentiate these moments and to convey the sense of filmed reality. In the production Ms. Silverman directed at The Women's Project, a live feed was used to film Dave's last speech with the onstage video camera, and Dave's video image was projected on a screen behind the actor.

MUSIC USE

Licensees are solely responsible for obtaining formal written permission from copyright owners to use copyrighted music in the performance of this play and are strongly cautioned to do so. If no such permission is obtained by the licensee, then the licensee must use only original music that the licensee owns and controls. Licensees are solely responsible and liable for all music clearances and shall indemnify the copyright owners of the play and their licensing agent, Samuel French, Inc., against any costs, expenses, losses and liabilities arising from the use of music by licensees.

ACT I

(PAUL enters the stage. Alone, he faces us. He hesitates. He tries to begin speaking. He stops, stammers. He finally manages.)

PAUL. *(facing out, addressing us directly)* **I don't know where to begin.**

(DAVE alone in a separate, brightly lit space.)

DAVE. The Tacoma Narrows Bridge was ruptured by wind and collapsed four months after its completion in 1940.

PAUL. *(out)* **I keep looking for some time, some event, some moment ... *the* moment.**

DAVE. It had a twenty-eight hundred foot span.

PAUL. *(out)* **Not just a place to start, but the reason it all unwound in the way that it did.**

DAVE. It had weight, gravity, and pressure, while at the same time evoking ....

PAUL. *(out)* **The "inciting incident," I guess that's how it's ... called ....**

DAVE. ... flight.

PAUL. *(out)* **... the, um, "trigger."**

DAVE. Was it less beautiful to behold for proving unable to withstand the forces of nature?

PAUL. *(out)* **Rewind. Rewind.** *(Darkness on DAVE.)* **I mean, beginnings don't even exist until you get to the end and can start looking back, do they? It is ever really possible to pinpoint a**

7

moment— a single moment— When everything is about 'to change—you just don't know it yet? *(PAUL changes direction. Everything gets brighter.)* Maybe it began with a promise. The one I made to Dave a long time ago, before I knew he meant to take me up on it someday. The one I made and never thought about again, not until after. *(DAVE enters air-guitaring.)* End of high-school, beginning of life: the future spread out before us, an infinite picnic: limitless, certain, and bright. I anticipated inevitable greatness – for both of us.

(DAVE leaps onto a couch as PAUL crosses to join him. Music rises to full-blast, something like Steely Dan's "Any World." PAUL joins DAVE in the past.)

DAVE. The thing that's brilliant, the thing that's absofuck-inglutely brilliant is that he whines melodically.

PAUL. *(Not hearing over the music; to DAVE.)* What?

DAVE. The music. His music is like a whine. He's just this whiny guy who turns whining into poetry.

PAUL. *(To DAVE.)* WHAT?!

DAVE. *(Lowering the volume.)* That guy is a whiner.

PAUL. You know the guy?

DAVE. I'm talking about the musical whine. It's fucking genius, to raise whining to the level of an operatic art form. *(DAVE listens for a moment.)* Check it out: there's an insipid whine, a plaintive howl, an existential complaint.

PAUL. The word is "kvetch," Dude.

(DAVE sings along to the music for a stanza or two.)

DAVE. Whine, whine, whine. Who's stopping you from having your way, nasal boy?

PAUL. You're so high.

DAVE. I wish.

Annnh

PAUL. You just did a bong, Dude.

DAVE. The bong was empty, Dude.

PAUL. I saw you sucking up the smoke, Dude.

DAVE. I got a hit of plastic is all I got.

PAUL. So of our time.

DAVE. To fill yourself with plastic.

PAUL. The only molecule grouping without a smell.

DAVE. You're telling me plastic doesn't have a smell? Have you never smelled burning plastic?

PAUL. Everything has a smell when it burns. In its inert state, plastic is like completely smell-less.

DAVE. There is a definite plastic smell and a plastic taste.

PAUL. You are so wrong, my friend.

DAVE. Haven't you ever had a sip of plastic-y water? When it's been in a plastic container for a while, what is that taste, if not plastic?

PAUL. *(Licking the plastic bong.)* Nada. Steely Dan was the name of their bong, you know.

DAVE. *(Making game show buzz sound.)* Annnh. Sorry, it was a dildo.

PAUL. Bong.

DAVE. Dildo.

PAUL. Bong.

DAVE. Dildo.

PAUL. A hundred bucks.

DAVE. Fuck off. Burroughs, Naked Lunch, dildo, try reading the classics, Dude. *(DAVE licks the bong.)* This is wild ... everything, even plastic, is emitting particles into the atmosphere. Everything is alive, Paulie, even dead matter. Maybe plastic takes a breath, like, every million years or so, it's metabolism is so slow that we humans, with our limited capabilities, we never even see it.

PAUL. I'm hungry.

DAVE. Or maybe this plastic is taking a breath in imperceptible milliseconds too rapid for us to measure.

PAUL. I am so hungry I'm gonna die.

DAVE. I just had a scientific breakthrough, Paulie. Some things are in fast motion and some things are in slow motion and therefore most of life, most of life, 'cause it's on a different speed setting than we are, is just this indistinguishable, undetectable blur.

PAUL. I'm having a salt craving and a sweet craving simultaneously.

DAVE. I'm gonna end up a bum, Paulie.

PAUL. You already are a bum.

DAVE. I'm serious, Sellars.

PAUL. Senior slump is to be expected.

DAVE. What if I never get out of the slump.

PAUL. We're not gonna be bums. Unless someday bums *rule* the fucking world!

DAVE. *(Energized.)* I just got a glimpse, a glimpse of the future, life after high school, and I am such a fucking bum, man. Someday, someday when everyone is putting on their three-piece suits and ties, including you, Dude, and driving to their big-shot jobs in their big ol' Buicks and shaking hands and smoking cigars and winning, like, Good Citizen Awards from the Rotary Club and driving their kids to Little League and whatever shit, I'll still be sitting on some couch somewhere, except the couch'll be really ratty and smell like cat piss, probably in some five-bucks-an-hour motel, and you'll have forgotten about me except to think once in awhile "Poor David Hummer, have you heard what a sorry bum the guy turned out to be?"

PAUL. You already got into the brand-name schools, Loser. The world is our freakin' dime bag.

DAVE. Don't leave me behind, Paulie.

PAUL. Nah, I'll drop off the kids at Grandma's and swing by your piss-stink motel to hang and smoke some weed with my old buddy Dave.

DAVE. Don't leave me to the goddamn werewolves. Don't let me die a sorry-ass bum in a stinking motel room.

PAUL. When I'm President, I'll make you my Secretary of

State.

DAVE. I'm not joking, Paulie. You gotta keep me off the ratty couch. Promise. Promise me. You gotta promise me.

PAUL. Whatever, Hummer.

(DAVE pins PAUL down.)

DAVE. Say it.

(DAVE grabs PAUL's wrist with surprising force.)

PAUL. Yeah, sure, I promise. God. *(As he stands.)* Whatever.

(PAUL shakes himself and comes forward. DAVE stays still for a moment, letting PAUL create the distance between them.)

PAUL. *(out)* **The purpose of pull-back retraction, moving the camera further and further away, is to distance oneself emotionally from the subject at hand.** *(DAVE backs away into darkness as PAUL speaks:)* **It's always been my favorite camera technique. And sometimes, sometimes when you pull back far enough, you reveal something else on screen, something that the frame was just missing.**

(Lights up on KAREN seated at a café table. She reads a thick book, making notes as she goes.)

PAUL. *(Approaching KAREN.)* Are you interested in, um … *(Reading title.)* The lives of saints?

KAREN. *(Evenly, going back to her book.)* No.

PAUL. Oh. Just reading about them, then?

KAREN. Right.

PAUL. Wow, that's, that's amazing, to read such a thick

book about a subject in which you have no particular, um— *(She looks up now, straight at him.)* I know this sounds like a really stupid line, but ... you look familiar. Really. Sincerely. I'm sorry, I should—

KAREN. We had a meeting. I had an idea for a movie. I tried to sell you the idea.

PAUL. That's it.

KAREN. *(Standing.)* And I promised myself that if I ever saw you again I would have the wherewithal to tell you what a colossal asshole you were.

PAUL. Oh.

KAREN. Which I wasn't going to do because after all this time, I don't exactly care anymore, not nearly as much as I thought I would, but since you asked ....

PAUL. I want to apologize. I do apologize. Just tell me what exactly I'm apologizing for and I'll be extremely contrite.

KAREN. Really, if you can't remember, don't worry about it.

(KAREN starts to go.)

PAUL. I can't remember because I was no doubt dazzled by your beauty. And intelligence.

(KAREN stops. Looks at him for a moment. With as much charm as she can muster:)

KAREN. Okay, if you really want, you can apologize for making me feel like a complete fool for being so pretentious and absurd as to deign to pitch you a piece of literature, an update of Dostoevsky's The Idiot, if that rings a bell ... for making me feel ashamed to care about Dostoevsky, about literature in general, though I suppose treating me like a pathetic desperate loser gave you a lot of satisfaction because in some sense I remind you of the girls who wouldn't even consider going out with you in high school, and in that way I've forgiven and even pitied you.

      PAUL. Um....

      KAREN. Bye-bye. Nice seeing you again.

      PAUL. *(Calling after her as she goes.)* Wait, how can I ... what's your name? *(out)* **That's all it took— *(She's gone.)* I was in love.** *(PAUL turns to DAVE, who is planted on a couch.)* This girl, this girl is so sexy, Dave. She's one of those super-smart intensoids who used to intimidate me, but I am so ready, you know? I am so sick of the melters, the girls who lose their fucking minds when they're with you; suddenly your hobbies are their hobbies, your opinions are their opinions, your plaid shirts are on their backs all the time—like what happened to the interesting person I met, you know? *(DAVE doesn't respond.)* I'm glad you're here, Dave. It's good to see you, man. My couch is your couch, okay? Stay as long as you want.

      DAVE. I can't do it anymore.

      PAUL. Do what?

      DAVE. *(Dryly, not without humor.)* Wake up. Get out of bed. Wash my face. Brush my teeth. Take off my clothes. Get in the shower. Wash the body. Wash the hair. Dry off the hair, dry off the body. Put on boxers. Put on pants. Put on shirt. Watch band. Buckle it. Three separate steps involved just in buckling it. Buttons. Buttons, man. Ten buttons. On average. Counting two per sleeve. Isn't that a lot of buttons to have to button and unbutton every single day of your life?

      PAUL. You're wearing a T-shirt.

      DAVE. That's why. The socks. The shoes. The laces. The laces that have to be tied. And that's just the first hour of the day.

      PAUL. It takes you an hour to get dressed?

      DAVE. If I get dressed. If I bother. If I go through all those mind-numbingly repetitious relentless never-ending meaningless steps. Every single day, only to be undone again at night, only to start over again by day, undone at night, start again by day ....

      PAUL. It's not that big of a deal, Dave.

      DAVE. We're all like Penelope at the goddamn spinning

wheel, you know what I'm saying?

PAUL. I happen to enjoy my little morning rituals, my morning ablutions.

DAVE. Weaving and unweaving, weaving and unweaving ....

PAUL. I appreciate a routine.

DAVE. Is there a *point* to any of this or does one indeed just light up a *joint*?

(DAVE starts to light up a joint.)

PAUL. Do you really think you should be doing that?

DAVE . *(Ignoring him.)* The question remains: what am I doing with my life?

PAUL. Breaking in my couch.

DAVE. Exactly. I am back, back on your couch.

PAUL. You're writing a novel.

DAVE. Just what the world needs, another novel. That's exactly what's missing—not enough novels to go around.

PAUL. You're depressing the hell out of me, Dave. Have you thought about getting a job?   DAVE. Now there's a novel idea.

PAUL. A little social interaction in the workaday world would not be such a terrible thing.

DAVE. A novel idea to replace writing of novel, for which I have *no* ideas.

PAUL. We're going out.

DAVE. You want to go find her?

PAUL. I don't even know her name.

DAVE. She'll return eventually. We are all creatures of habit, of desperately clung-to forces of familiarity.

PAUL. What if she thinks I'm a stalker?

DAVE. You are. I'll be there to reassure her that you're the good kind of stalker.

PAUL. *(out)* **Cut to the café. Not a very elegant cut.**

Completely predictable and mundane. That's okay, I think most people like to know where they're going. You set up a cafe scene, they feel cheated if you suddenly show them, say, a three-ring circus.

(PAUL starts for the café. Before he can get there, a detour. Flashback: KAREN holds a paperback copy of The Idiot as she pitches it.)

KAREN. Yes, *The Idiot* is long.

(PAUL takes KAREN in.)

PAUL. *(out and to KAREN)* **People, in my experience, generally don't like detours.**

KAREN. It's long because it's full of tangents. Really wonderful tangents. Which I think could be interesting. Because, because that's only a problem if you have a single destination in mind, and aren't willing to change it.

(KAREN tosses PAUL the paperback as she goes.)

PAUL. *(out)* **The Idiot. A book I still haven't read all the way through and, it's probably safe to say, never will. I bought it only because of a girl who, when I first encountered her, I had somehow failed to notice.** *(The café. DAVE is jotting something down. PAUL flips through* The Idiot. *To DAVE.)* If she doesn't show up soon I may wind up actually reading this thing. *(DAVE ignores him, focused.)* Dave? What are you writing there, Dave?

DAVE. There is definitely a statistical connection between impaired vision and tea drinkers.

PAUL. What?

DAVE. That guy just ordered tea. Third guy in glasses to order tea. Red, however, wearing the color red seems to correspond somehow with frappadappaccino drinking. That is a frappadappaccino

Red Jacket is drinking, isn't it?

       PAUL. I don't know, Dave. I don't care. What's with this list shit?

       DAVE. If we average out what everyone orders vis-à-vis physical attributes and style choices, we can predict what this person you like will most likely order and order it ahead *for* her thereby totally ingratiating ourselves with our perspicacity.

       PAUL. That's absurd.

       DAVE. So is weather forecasting, but it works. Uh oh, conundrum: 3 o'clock, individual attired in red jacket *and* eyeglasses.

       PAUL. You're losing it, Dave.

       DAVE. *(After a beat.)* I am not *losing* "it." *(Standing.)* I never *had* "it." Unless your "it" and my "it" are diametrically opposed a la cappuccino vs. chamomile which, by the by, is closely tied to the wearing of earth tones in the generally mossy hues.

       PAUL. Can we calm down, please?

       DAVE. I came here to help you, remember? Try to remember that you are not helping me. I am helping you. You clearly have issues with that. Fuck you.

(DAVE gets up and goes. PAUL starts after him—)

       PAUL. Dave—

(KAREN sees PAUL.)

       KAREN. Oh.

(PAUL sees KAREN.)

       PAUL. Hi.

(PAUL turns to see what DAVE will do. DAVE goes. KAREN sits. PAUL goes to her.)

PAUL. I ... never got your name.

KAREN. *(Wryly.)* Couldn't you look it up? "Old ideas pitched, thoroughly rejected, pitcher savagely humiliated"—there must be some kind of bin for that.

PAUL. I hated that job, I really completely—I'm sure I sabotaged every smart idea that came across my desk. *(Showing book.)* And I've been reading *The Idiot*, and it's a damn fine piece of literature—

KAREN. Please, I'm over it.

PAUL. *(As she goes off, he remembers.)* Karen. God. It's like getting stuck on the 7th dwarf; I've been going nuts trying to think of it—

KAREN. Doc.

PAUL. Sorry?

KAREN. One tends to forget Doc. Doc or Dopey.

PAUL. I'd never forget Dopey. *(Extending hand.)* Paul Sellars.

KAREN. I know. I never forget an enemy.

PAUL. Nice trait. Would you ... care to join the enemy for a cup of peace-making tea in neutral territory, Karen—Sanderson? *(KAREN sits at PAUL's table. An awkward pause.)* So—are you still writing screenplays?

KAREN. I never really was. Actually writing them. I was pitching them.

PAUL. And very well, I might add.

KAREN. *(Cutting him off.)* I never sold anything. I was completely stupid about it. I've gone back to school.

PAUL. *(Overly enthusiastic.)* That's fantastic.

KAREN. Is it?

PAUL. *(Again, too eager.)* I think that's awesome.

KAREN. Less expensive than trying to sell screenplays, anyway.

PAUL. How's that?

KAREN. As a grad student, you figure out how to get by on the little you make teaching instead of counting on the promise of that big Hollywood pay-day that's sure to come any day now.

PAUL. What are you studying?

KAREN. You know, I only agreed to let you sit here so I could watch you eat crow.

PAUL. Ah.

KAREN. And yet I'm having trouble mustering up the hatred I thought I felt for you. *(Getting up.)* Good luck, Paul. Really.

PAUL. How about dinner? I mean if you're available. I don't even know if you're available. *(She doesn't say anything. But she doesn't go.)* It could be an extremely quick dinner, like, sushi bar or something, we don't even have to face each other. And I hear their special crow maki is excellent.

KAREN. The thing is, after that pitch I spent a lot of time complaining to my friends about what a jerk you were, so I could never actually go on a date with you.

PAUL. *(out)* **Life as a series of jump cuts, artificially connected by theme or the element of surprise. "I will never, ever, ever feed elephants at the zoo," smash cut to same feeding elephants at the zoo. "I wouldn't be caught dead wearing that chicken suit," jump cut to same still alive, wearing said chicken suit.** *(Pulling out a seat for KAREN.)* **I like artifice. And speed. And forward motion.**

(PAUL turns back to KAREN.)

KAREN. Hagiography.

PAUL. That is—biography of hags?

KAREN. Of saints, actually. "Holy writing." That's where the word comes from.

PAUL. They should come up with a new word, don't you think? Very misleading.

KAREN. I love words that sound like the opposite of what

they are.

PAUL. Why?

KAREN. *(Coy.)* Reminder not to trust first impressions.

PAUL. *(Beat.)* So you're writing a hago-bio sort of thing?

KAREN. I'm interested in biography that idealizes, even idolizes, its subject, using the hagiographic model. Uggh, I sound like such a grad student. I'm, um, writing about photographs. A bunch of photographs. As hago-bio sort of things. It's—I don't think you'll find it very interesting.

PAUL. I love saints.

KAREN. Oh?

PAUL. It's a Jewish thing. We're really into being martyrs. Or at least our mothers are; we probably don't have saints because they'd all think they deserve the honor.

KAREN. Virginia Oldoini wasn't much of a saint, as it happens. That's who I'm writing about—the Countess de Castiglione— have you heard of her?

PAUL. No, but I've always wanted to. Hear of her.

KAREN. She was considered a great beauty of her time. She considered herself a great beauty. She had herself photographed hundreds of times. This was in the mid-1800s, when photography was still pretty new, and the photos, she used the photos to preserve but also to alter reality, to in essence idealize herself—that's, um, that's kind of the thesis, anyway.

PAUL. I'll bet she had a really fascinating life.

KAREN. She went mad. Lost her beauty. Died a recluse.

PAUL. Oh. Well I'm sure there's a story in that, too.

KAREN. I hope so. The thing that interests me is the collaboration with her photographer—it lasted over forty years.

PAUL. Have you thought about pitching that?

KAREN. Pitching what?

PAUL. The Countess and the Photographer. I see a movie in that.

KAREN. As I said, I'm not interested in movies anymore. I

thought you'd given up that line of work, too. Being pitched to.

   PAUL. I want to direct. That sounds like a joke, right? "What I really want to do is direct." But that's what I was setting out to do before I got sidetracked by all that development executive crap. I went to film school. That job was a minor detour.

   KAREN. No wonder you seemed frustrated.

   PAUL. What can I tell you, I was an idiot.

   KAREN. Not worthy of that label. *(Off PAUL's look.)* In a world made of idiots, it's the one true and pure and genuine soul who's perceived as such.

(PAUL is putty in her hands. He turns to DAVE.)

     PAUL. What can I say, she was putty in my hands.
     DAVE. Well done.
     PAUL. Ol' Paul Sellars has still got the touch.

(DAVE points out a grocery bag.)

     DAVE. I got you some groceries.
     PAUL. Thanks, Dave.
     DAVE. Thanks for putting me up.

(DAVE hands PAUL the grocery bag. PAUL looks inside. He takes out a tin of baking powder.)

     PAUL. Baking powder?
     DAVE. Isn't that a great tin? *(PAUL takes out another identical tin.)* I love that tin.

(Another tin. And another. They keep coming, a couple dozen in all.)

     PAUL. What is this?
     DAVE . You can never have too much baking powder.

PAUL. Yes, you can, Dave.

DAVE. It's really classic, this tin. It's like the whole history of American cookery on this one little label. It's got a million uses.

PAUL. Baking soda.

DAVE. What?

PAUL. I think you're confusing baking powder and baking soda. Not that I'd want a bag full of baking soda, either.

DAVE. You don't like it.

PAUL. Dave, I ....

DAVE. You don't like my gift. You want me out of here. Just say it.

PAUL. I don't want you out of here.

DAVE. I'm in the way.

PAUL. You're not in the way.

DAVE. Would you tell me if I were in the way?

PAUL. You're not.

DAVE. By the way, Vivian called.

PAUL. Shit, Vivian. You didn't say anything?

DAVE. I said *some*thing. I couldn't just breathe heavily.

PAUL. You know what I mean, Dave. Did you tell her where I was?

DAVE. You didn't tell me to lie.

PAUL. I don't want you to lie, but you didn't have to mention— DAVE. It's not like you're overlapping.

PAUL. That's right. I'm not. I told you, it's been shit with Vivian.

DAVE. Does Vivian know that?

PAUL. How could she not know that?

DAVE. She sounded sad.

PAUL. She's a sad person.

DAVE. Maybe you made her sad.

PAUL. Dave, it's been over with her for months.

DAVE. Because it lost the jolt of the new. That zing. That ping. That special thing. But then you kept her around, kept her hang-

ing around hoping it could still work out, until you could come up
with someone new.

      PAUL. She told you this?

      DAVE. I know you, Paul, she didn't have to.

      PAUL. You run through women, too.

      DAVE. I don't lie to them. I just can't seem to keep them.

      PAUL. You run through women, Dave. No, I take that back,
you run away from them.

      DAVE. I run away from women? *Mais, j'adore les femmes.*

      PAUL. Do you tell them? Do you?

      DAVE. What are you saying?

      PAUL. What I am saying, what I am saying is— *(out)* **Flash
back. Back. Keep going back. Think high eighties, last year of
college: girls in shoulder pads and big hair, men in banker suspenders or Converse high tops. Suspenders *and* high tops.**

(A pop of light. DAVE is on the telephone.)

      DAVE. *(Picking up phone.)* I need to talk to the President.
Yes, the President of the United States, you heard me. What does it
take to get through here? Fuck you, the planetary realignment is going
to be on your head, then, on your head.

(DAVE slams down the phone.)

      PAUL. *(Entering the flashback.)* What's going on, Dave?

      DAVE. Whose side are you on? Whose side are you on,
that's what I want to know.

      PAUL. You are so wired.

      DAVE. The whole place is wired.

      PAUL. You need to sleep.

      DAVE. We're being set up but you don't even see it.

      PAUL. You never sleep anymore.

      DAVE. You don't even *see* what they are trying to *do* and I know, and they know I know.

PAUL. This isn't funny.

DAVE. No, it isn't. It's a nightmare. A living nightmare. I saw Saturn last night, I got a good look at Saturn, and it's a lot closer to us than you think.

PAUL. What are you on?

DAVE. Don't you see what they're doing?

PAUL. Did you take something?

DAVE. They're moving the planet, the whole planet, that's what NASA is up to these days, and I don't think we can survive if they do that, I don't think we can, I need to warn people, no one knows what is going on.

PAUL. What did you take?

DAVE. Stay away from me—

PAUL. Dave—

DAVE. What have you done to me, don't touch me, don't fucking touch me—

PAUL . Calm down, Dave, just calm down.

DAVE. Ahhh! These clothes are strangling me!

PAUL. Just calm the fuck down.

(DAVE starts to try to tear off his clothes.)

DAVE. Why are they doing this to me?

PAUL. You need to relax, okay?

DAVE. Help me, Paulie!

PAUL. Sit down and breathe.

DAVE. They've wired my whole body. I've got to get out of my body. Help me, somebody, I am Jesus Fucking Christ help me Father help me oh Lord and Savior help me DAD!

(Flashback over. A pop of light as the scene shifts back.)

DAVE. I run away from women? *Mais, j'adore les femmes.*

PAUL. Do you tell them? Do you?

DAVE. What are you saying?

PAUL. What I am saying, what I am saying is—do you tell them, or do you just give them a gentle little shove out of your life before you have to?

DAVE. What do you want me to do, get a big fat scarlet L tattooed on my chest? Lunatic.

PAUL. You know I don't think that.

DAVE. Feel free to substitute Loser.

PAUL. I never even think about it.

DAVE. Me neither. Oh, it does come up a bit at my weekly with my therapist and my spot checks with my psychopharmacologist and my 15-pill-a-day yummy snack packs and my intermittent holidays at the hospital ward—okay, I guess I do think about it.

PAUL. I'm sorry, Dave. I just want you to be happy.

DAVE. I want you to be happy. I'm sorry, man. I do, I do want you to be happy.

(They hug.)

PAUL. Be happy, man.

DAVE. Do whatever it takes to be happy.

PAUL. We are so queer.

DAVE. We are so custard. I love you, man. I'm sorry I'm crazy.

PAUL. You're not crazy. You wanna talk crazy? Me falling in love, that's what's crazy.

DAVE. Are you falling "madly" in love?

(A pop of light. PAUL turns to KAREN. He unbuttons her shirt as she speaks.)

KAREN. The Countess became more and more interested in painted photographs when she realized it allowed her to control the finished product—her own form.

PAUL. Mmm.

KAREN. Which sometimes meant disguising it, camouflaging perceived shortcomings—either painting over the image herself, or directing the photography studio's well, touch-up artists is what they were; even though the camera seemed more truthful it was actually a way to manipulate the, um—You really want to hear about this?

PAUL. Absolutely.

KAREN. If she thought the artist deserved the privilege of witnessing her perfection, she was willing to expose her body.

PAUL. Tell me more.

KAREN. Well, there are these shots of her feet. And her legs. The frame cut off just above the knee. Very scandalous at the time. I should show you—

PAUL. Sex.

KAREN. —do you want to see?

PAUL. *(out)* **Sex sex sex sex sex. Whenever Karen spoke, all I could think about was sex. When we were together, when we were apart, I had one thing on my mind: sex. Except when we had sex.** *(Breaking away from KAREN.)* **When we had sex I had distractions. For some reason I had trouble being completely there.**

KAREN. Paul? You seem distracted.

PAUL. It's—I wish you didn't have a roommate.

KAREN. I wish you didn't have one.

PAUL. You know he's not exactly a roommate. He's more like a couch guest.

KAREN. For how long?

PAUL. Till he gets back on his feet.

KAREN. He's been off his feet?

PAUL. His feet, they aren't the most stable feet. I guess you should know, he's— *(out)* **Here it comes. The first betrayal of many betrayals.** *(To KAREN.)* —kind of crazy. You should know he's kind of crazy.

KAREN. "Kind of crazy"?

PAUL. I'm just saying he's a little nuts. *(out)* **Maybe, maybe I was afraid she'd like him better than me. Most women did.**

KAREN. We're all a little nuts.

PAUL. No, he's really—I know "crazy" is a very un-PC word to use. It's … manic depression.

KAREN. That's it? Why are you making such a big deal out of manic depression?

PAUL. Do you have it, too? Because some of my best friends—in fact my actual best friend—

KAREN. Almost all of the artists I like had it.

PAUL. *(out)* **Had I unwittingly just given out points in his favor?** *(To KAREN.)* I just thought it was something you should know.

KAREN. I'm sure I know lots of people with manic depression, and I don't even know it.

PAUL. In this case, I thought you should know.

(A pop of light. DAVE, KAREN, and PAUL sit down to dinner.)

DAVE. So Paulie's probably warned you about me.

(Before KAREN can respond:)

PAUL. That's right, I told her you hit on all my girlfriends.

KAREN. Hmm, how many girlfriends are we talking about here?

PAUL. Tell him about the Countess, Karen. Karen's a sort of, um, hago-biogra-photographer.

DAVE. He probably told you I'm crazy.

KAREN. Sorry?

DAVE. Don't let him turn you into a liar, Karen. You're better than that, I can tell.

PAUL. Dave, can we try to enjoy ourselves here?

DAVE. What did he tell you about me? Hmmm?

PAUL. Wait till you try this salad dressing.

KAREN. He said you were best friends from the age of seven.

DAVE. That's it?

PAUL. I made the salad dressing myself. The secret is rice vinegar.

KAREN. I don't stigmatize a chemical imbalance, if that's what you're getting at.

DAVE. Oh, an enlightened one.

PAUL. Karen says all of the great artists—a lot of them anyway—tell him, Karen.

DAVE. Yes, tell him. Oh, wait, was there an added degree of hysteria in those words? Did you detect an edge of paranoia, an inappropriate and aggressive inflection?

KAREN. Nothing beyond the normal range for this situation.

DAVE. And we all want very much to be normal.

PAUL. Okay, Dave.

DAVE. Have I veered over the line yet? Tipped the needle ever so slightly? Please tell me so I can be as normal as you someday.

KAREN. I'm sorry.

PAUL. Don't be sorry, you didn't do anything.

KAREN. I didn't mean to offend you.

DAVE. You haven't offended me at all. I like you, Karen. I think you're pretty, sweet, and very good for our friend Paul.

KAREN. Thanks. But is he good for me?

DAVE. Pretty, sweet, and smart. Smart enough to look in between the words now, no? Knowing what you know about me and my mental condition, everything I say is loaded, oozing with the possibilities of my intermittent madness. "Is it coming on yet? Is he having a spell of it?" Don't worry, I look at myself that way now, too ... it's fantastic, the way there are so many added layers of interest whenever I lift my fork to eat—will I stab myself, stab you, miss my mouth completely the way crazy people do sometimes? Have you ever noticed that, the way crazy old ladies have their lipstick on over here, on their cheek, like they can't see where the opening of their mouth is…. Much more exciting, isn't it, to have the possibilities of discourse expanded this way?

PAUL. Are you pleased with yourself?

DAVE. Yes, I am. Not in a self-aggrandizing, delusional way, I hope.

KAREN. You're funny.

DAVE. You think so?

KAREN. I do.

DAVE. You must be laughing on the inside.

KAREN. I do all my best emotions there.

(DAVE and KAREN smile at each other.)

PAUL. Okay then. This is good. This is okay. We're all internally laughing here.

(A pop of light as KAREN goes.)

DAVE. She's great.

PAUL. You like her?

DAVE. I love her.

PAUL. You like her?

DAVE. I love her.

PAUL. That's so cool you like her.

DAVE. I really do like her. Do you think she liked me?

PAUL. Definitely, she definitely liked you, too, I could tell. *(out)* **Having a best friend on your couch is strangely … empowering. A buffer between yourself and the world, a catalyst to motion. On the couch, Dave reminded me that I was not on the couch. Things that I had been afraid of saying or doing, I suddenly did.** *(Turning to KAREN.)* I was thinking, would you want to live together?

KAREN. "Would" I?

PAUL. Maybe you should move in with me.

KAREN. You mean with you and Dave.

PAUL. For the time being. He doesn't take up much space. He's very inactive. You have to find a new apartment anyway.

KAREN. So this is a real estate decision?

PAUL. Don't ruin a romantic moment. I've been working up to this moment.

KAREN. Romantic? Really?

PAUL. I've never asked anyone before. I want you to live with me, Karen. I know this is fast, but move in with me, see how it goes.

KAREN. Oh, yes, now that does sound romantic: "see how it goes."

PAUL. And then we can start looking for a place together.

KAREN. *If* it goes well.

PAUL. Don't you want to see how it goes, too?

KAREN. I'm sorry, but I don't think moving in together is a see-how-it-goes proposition. I think it's a turn my life upside-down, put my faith and my hope and my esteem in the hands of another human being, sacrifice my independence and my freedom and my self-sufficiency which I am willing to do on a leap, as an act belief, but not as a dare or a gamble or a see-how-it-goes what-the-hell.

PAUL. So I guess the answer would be no.

(A pop of light. KAREN faces us.)

KAREN. *(out)* **I always wanted to be on of those what-the-hell girls ... you know the ones I mean ... they usually have a little tattoo of, say, a dolphin on their ankle that they got on the spur of the moment when it was trendy, what-the-hell. They smoke cigs and drink too much, what-the-hell. They've all been with other women, even the straight ones, what-the-hell. They're sexy, despite their usually stringy hair and unmade-up faces, because they think they are, and they're young as shit, and skinny,** and they live with this guy and then that guy without losing faith, or innocence, or pride, what the hell great way to save on rent and hey, it's fun for a while, cool and carefree and shit I am just not, have never been, carefree.

(A pop of light as KAREN returns to the scene with PAUL.)

KAREN. *(To PAUL.)* I will move in with you, Paul, what the hell. Until I can find my own place at least. But I want you to know that I didn't ruin a romantic moment. It was more like a toaster-oven moment. A blender moment. A perfectly utilitarian non-moment. Okay?

PAUL. *(out)* **Sometimes, looking back, I think the truth is that Karen and I never really got along at all.**

KAREN. You look nice, you know.

PAUL. You think so? *(out)* **But maybe I'm remembering it wrong. Remembering the bad more than the good, the way you only keep a diary on the lousy days.**

KAREN. Very dashing. I would definitely give this man a budget and a crew.

PAUL. I want this job. I need this job. Unfortunately the smell of desperation is never a good thing.

KAREN. You smell perfect. You'll be perfect. You are perfect.

PAUL. "Perfect"? Hmmm. You are very good at hagiographizing.

KAREN. Not with him around. I can't—does he do anything other than lie around on the couch, order take-out food and let his dishes pile up in the sink without thinking about who'll wash them?

PAUL. Why don't you work at the library today?

KAREN. He never writes, you know. That novel he claims to be working on?

PAUL. *(out)* **I always knew when Karen's own writing wasn't going well.**

KAREN. He never fucking is.
PAUL. *(To KAREN.)* I'll talk to him.

(A pop of light. KAREN at the kitchen counter, trying to work, not working. DAVE calls to KAREN from the couch, where he lies with remote control in one hand, bag of chips in the other.)

DAVE. *(calling from couch.)* K, come see this, you gotta check this out! *(KAREN approaches.)* I love these nature shows. Nature is so fucking freaky.

KAREN. You should get off the couch.

DAVE. What?

KAREN. The couch. You spend too much time on it.

DAVE. Already sick of having me around. I blame you not. I'm sick of having me around.

KAREN. Then get up.

DAVE. Easy for you to say. I didn't want to tell anybody, but I've got glue on my ass ....

KAREN. Get the fuck up, get off the fucking couch and do something with your life! *(Startled by her own outburst.)* Sorry.

DAVE. No, no you're right. I really should.

KAREN. I'm so sorry. It's none of my business, I—I don't know why I—

DAVE. It's okay, K. Tell me off. Really, say whatever's on your mind.

KAREN. We all feel like shit, okay? We all feel like lying on the couch and not getting up but we do it. We fucking well do it. Your life is slipping by, you, you loser.

DAVE. Well done.

KAREN. God, I'm such a—

(DAVE makes room on the couch. KAREN sits.)

DAVE. It's really okay. I'm trying to get up. Get up off the couch. I'm working on it.... I think my foot's asleep. Maybe my whole body.

KAREN. It's me. I'm the loser.

DAVE. No, I agree with you completely. I mean, not that you're a loser. That I am. *(Trying to get off the couch, exaggerating his stuck-ness.)* That I must get off this couch, that that is absolutely— essential, a really damn fine— *(He can't get up. Sinks back into the couch.)* —idea.

KAREN. I see you on the couch, lying around eating chips, and, and I hate chips but I, I just think it makes so much more sense than what I'm doing.

DAVE. I'm poisoning you with my inertia.

KAREN. I'm already inert. What do I have to say about the Countess de Castiglione that hasn't been said already anyway? She lived. She was considered very beautiful. She had a lot of pictures of herself taken. She died. Beauty fades. I'm boring myself. I'm boring Paul, too.

DAVE. Paul's mad for you, K. And believe you me, I know from mad.

KAREN. Not me. He fell for someone else.

DAVE. That's crazy. And believe you me I know from crazy.

KAREN. Not another woman; another version. A fake. Not the real me, but my own impostor.

DAVE. We're a little club of dualities here.

KAREN. Don't you see? I completely misrepresented my-self.

DAVE. I knew it; C.I.A. operative?

KAREN. I made it seem like I'm a person unafraid of telling people off, a person who can stand up for herself without the slightest concern of whether or not she will be liked. And that's the person whom Paul fancies. But doing that ... telling him off the way I did when we first hooked up ... that was completely unlike me.

DAVE. You just told *me* off.

KAREN. I'm really sorry about that.

DAVE. Fairly well, I might add.

KAREN. So apparently I'm a person capable of intermittent outbursts that go way beyond what is appropriate due to my more usual inability to confront and express what I am feeling at all.

DAVE. "Appropriate" is my least favorite word.

(KAREN bursts into tears.)

KAREN. Sorry. I'm sorry.

DAVE. If you're seated next to someone who starts to cry on an airplane, say, would you give them a hug, A; B, hand them a hankie; C, ignore out of not wishing to embarrass the said sobber?

KAREN. I don't know. Ignore, I think. Ignore sympathetically, if possible.

DAVE. Strangers are easier to comfort somehow than acquaintances, than friends of friends, maybe strangers are even easier than friends.

KAREN. I don't know.

DAVE. Really, friends are the hardest, if you're not used to being the one who comforts. *(DAVE puts an arm around her to comfort. Pats her on the back a bit awkwardly. She stands. He stands and gives her a hug. They sway back and forth.)* We're dancing.

KAREN. Swaying.

DAVE. Feels like dancing.

KAREN. There's no music.

DAVE. Music would be redundant.

(They sway another moment.)

KAREN. You're off the couch.

(They continue to sway. PAUL enters.)

PAUL. Hi. Whatcha doing?

DAVE. Dancing, Paul.

KAREN. Can't you see we're dancing?

PAUL. There isn't any music.

KAREN. That's what you think.

DAVE. Come dance with us, Paulie.

KAREN. Yes, dance with us.

PAUL. Tell me you two aren't having an affair and we'll move on.

DAVE. Having enough air?

KAREN. We're not having an affair, Paul.

PAUL. Good. Because I got the commercial.

KAREN. You got it?

PAUL. I shouldn't say anything because it's not completely official and you know how these things can go away but—I got it.

(PAUL knocks on the wood table.)

DAVE. You know when you do that, you're knocking on the cross. The symbolic cross. That's where knocking on wood comes from. Do you mean to knock on a symbolic cross?

KAREN. That's interesting, I didn't know that.

PAUL. Very interesting, yeah, so can you believe it? My first real directing gig, not just some low-brow industrial.

DAVE. No, this would be a high-brow donut commercial.

PAUL. I—okay, but this is a really cool spot, Dave.

DAVE. I'm sure you'll do something very clever and profound with the donut footage, but isn't there a hole in the middle of this whole thing?

PAUL. People would kill for this job.

DAVE. You know what I think of people. Especially people who kill. If you keep taking every shitty little job that comes your way, you'll never get the chance to do something that really means something to you.

PAUL. This isn't a shitty little job. This is a shitty big job.

It's not shitty at all, this job.

DAVE. It has nothing to do with what you set out to do.

PAUL. Some of us have to work for a living. I can't live the way you live, Dave. Crashing on people's couches. Wanting to write novels and not. Doing it.

DAVE. I'm a poor subject for comparison.

PAUL. Oh, but wait, I guess there's that tidy little trust fund of yours to ease your pain.

DAVE. If you want to get into that, it's not a trust fund. It's an *un*-trust fund. A lack of faith fund. A *disability* fund is more like it. A tiny *disability* fund because it was determined by my father before he died that I don't have the proper *abilities* to *succeed* in this particular life of mine, and you are welcome to it, Paul. Because you can still make your father proud. And I can't. I gave him no pride. I gave him worries. *(to PAUL.)* I'll give you money to make what you want.

PAUL. I don't want your money.

DAVE. A personal investment from your friend Dave who believes that Paul Sellars has something to say about something more than donuts.

PAUL. You wouldn't understand. Sorry I got a little bit psyched and thought you guys might actually be happy for me. But how unbecoming, to hustle for a job, to put yourself out there, to actually want to succeed—what a terrible trait, a genetic defect no doubt.

KAREN. I'm happy for you.

PAUL. You are?

KAREN. Of course I am. I think it's great.

PAUL. You do?

KAREN. Really great. All the big directors do commercials, and, and I love commercials. They're so much better than the shows. I even love donuts.

DAVE. Paulie hates donuts.

PAUL. That's right, Dave. It's a job. Unlike you, I happen to live in the real world.

DAVE. Oh, whoa, all this crap, and you're telling me it ain't even real? If it's not real the fucking joke's on me, man. Who gets to decide what's "real," by the by? Please inform.

(DAVE begins to sing an older song, something like Steely Dan's "Your Gold Teeth.")

> PAUL. We are not in high school anymore, Dave. Life is not a Steely Dan tune.
> DAVE. I do nut agree. Or is it I donut agree. Of course, I am a nut, so whenever I do something I do nut it.

(DAVE goes back to singing, now at the top of his lungs.)

> PAUL. *(Over, trying to drown him out.)* Shut up. Shut the fuck up and get a life, get your own life, you crazy fuck!
> KAREN. *(Simultaneous to above.)* Stop it. Both of you. What is wrong with you?

(They all stop abruptly; PAUL stops shouting. A pause.)

> DAVE. Well, I'm crazy, and Paul—Paulie here's just a plain old pain in the ass.

(A pop of light. PAUL watches DAVE go, then turns back to face us.)

> PAUL. *(out)* **In second-grade our science teacher, Mr. Paige, gave us our first real introduction to the magic of movie-making: a film of a seed turning into a sprout turning into a stalk turning into a blooming flower. All in the span of 90 seconds, through the modern miracle of time-lapse photography. After that Dave and I would try desperately to catch a plant just at the moment it grew; to see, with our own unaided eyes, a little green hand pushing through a seed, a tiny leaf edging out from the stalk. We could never see it as it was happening; only after it had**

happened. We kept missing the moment. Why could the camera see what we ourselves, even if we watched patiently, for hours on end, couldn't?

KAREN. It's okay. He'll be okay.

PAUL. I thought he'd be happy for me.

KAREN. We should go out and celebrate—a real date, just the two of us.

PAUL. What am I supposed to do? Wallow in obscurity so Dave can approve of my motives?

KAREN. Maybe he's afraid you'll leave us behind. Him behind.

PAUL. That's ridiculous.

KAREN. He wants to see you get to do what you want to do; but maybe he wants to be part of it, too.

PAUL. I want to make movies.

KAREN. Movies you care about.

PAUL. I care about my work. And I don't expect things to be handed to me, so if I have to pay my dues— But why am I justifying myself? Why do I care what he thinks? He's fucking—nuts.

(A pop of light. DAVE brightly lit in a separate space.)

DAVE. *(out)* Bipolar disorder with manic episodes usually lasting four to seven days and sometimes culminating in psychotic breaks with reality.

KAREN. Maybe you should make a movie about Dave.

PAUL. About Dave?

DAVE. *(out)* My manic episodes, at the rate of one every three to twelve months, are rather unpredictable. I love that they call them that: "episodes." Sounds like a TV series, doesn't it? My own little Gilligan's Island. At the end of every episode, I'm still stuck on this godforsaken island. Even though I can't escape, order has been restored.

KAREN. If you could take his life ...

DAVE. *(out)* **The problem is, in my show, I'm alone. No Skipper, no Professor and Mary Ann ... and where are the Howells when you need them, I must say ....**

KAREN. ... show what it's like. What it's really like, living with his illness; what he goes through.

PAUL. I'm sure it's been done.

KAREN. Everything's been done. You'll do it better.

PAUL. I thought you weren't interested in movies anymore.

KAREN. I'm not. I'm interested in you. And you're interested in Dave.

PAUL. You think Dave would be into it?

KAREN. He wants to help you.

PAUL. And maybe it would help him, too, do you think? To make this? To have something about him made?

DAVE. *(out)* **... Instead of a wooden raft—** *(Showing pills.)* **My little lifesavers. The problem is, every time I get better, I feel like I just don't need them anymore. Dr. V, Mom, and my best friend Paulie disagree. They know that my episodes are somewhat more frequent, prolonged, and severe than for most. Some people have only one episode in their whole lives; one episode, and they get off the island.**

(A pop of light. PAUL films DAVE.)

DAVE. *(To Paul's camera.)* Over the years, it's become apparent that I'm doomed to be a castaway forever. *(To KAREN and PAUL.)* So? What do you think?

KAREN. *(To PAUL.)* I think you should do this.

PAUL. We all should.

KAREN. What do you think, Dave?

PAUL. Because we think it could be great, but it's totally up to you.

DAVE. Seriously, guys, how's my hair?

END OF ACT ONE

ACT II

(PAUL films DAVE at breakfast.)

DAVE. *(Playing to the camera.)* His mouth fills with cereal. He crunches. He chews. He swallows. He takes a swig of juice. He takes a swag of pills. Another swig of juice. Man, is this fascinating or what? *(KAREN enters. Doing screenplay stage directions.)* Enter K. Beautiful. Sexy. Bed hair.

KAREN. Go away, too early.

DAVE. Cranky in that Julie Christie/Katherine Hepburn I-don't-give-a-damn but vulnerable underneath way.

(PAUL zooms in on KAREN.)

KAREN. Not on me, please.

PAUL. You're part of this.

KAREN. Turn the camera on yourself, then. You're part of this, too.

PAUL. Try to forget I'm here.

DAVE. That's too easy; give us a challenge, Paulie.

PAUL. Okay: be interesting.

DAVE. Nice. *(To camera.)* Meet Dave. An ordinary guy with manic depression, a.k.a. bipolar disorder, a.k.a. shit for brains. Make that scrambled brains. Brains a la coq. Brains Benedict, intermittently smothered in hollandaise. So, what's it like being Dave, Dave? Well, Dave, now that you ask, quite frankly, it quite often

sucks.
(A pop of light.)

PAUL. *(out)* The "McGuffin." Hitchcock's word for the seemingly insignificant object that actually becomes the central, um, reason for the plot to move forward. It might be a suitcase, or a cigarette lighter, or a missing jewel.

DAVE. *(out)* Lithium carbonate. An alkali metal, the salt of which seems to be a necessary and lacking component of my brain. A single dose at night and I am a new person. A well person. A better person, which means a person more like you of the naturally well-seasoned brain.

PAUL. *(out)* Can a movie's McGuffin be the ... camera itself? The decision to make the movie? Once we decided to make it, we had a beginning.

DAVE. *(out)* Yummy. Seventy to eighty percent of those in my category respond quite favorably to this lovely little pill. Side effects: weight gain, excessive thirst or urination, tremors, weakness, diarrhea, a metallic taste in the mouth, confusion, delirium, seizures, coma, and, rarely, death. Death as a side effect, I love that. And well worth it in my case.

PAUL. *(out)* Our triangle had a purpose.

(A pop of light. KAREN enters with a stack of papers and books.)

KAREN. *(Off papers.)* It says here that in some cultures, manic depressives are treated with respect and reverence.

DAVE. Where are these cultures? I'm on my way.

KAREN. Mainly in the past. But in the Ndungi tribe, mania is treated as a spiritual awakening— *(Reading.)* "The manic episode can be seen as a time when a human becomes closer to the god-self. "

DAVE. What does it say about manic shopping sprees?

KAREN. No mention.

DAVE. A disease exacerbated by credit card availability.

KAREN. Look at this list. "Writers, artists, and composers with probable major depression or manic depressive illness." *(Paul turns the camera on her.)* This list is amazing: Emily Dickinson. Victor Hugo. Lord Byron. *(Re camera.)* Oh, okay. *(To camera, self-consciously.)* Henry James. William James. Robert Lowell. Gustave Mahler. Hans Christian Anderson. I mean, you're in such good company. F. Scott Fitzgerald? T.S. Eliot. William Blake. Melville, Turgenev, Robert Luis Stevenson. Charles Mingus, Irving Berlin. Rachmaninoff. Michel*a*ngelo. Jesus, you start to think, who *doesn't* have it? Lots of great scientists have had it, too. That's a whole other list; I didn't print that one out.

DAVE. Yeah, who cares about scientists, not to mention all the other assorted anonymous schlubs. *(Off list.)* Hey, where's Hemingway?

KAREN. I didn't print out the suicides.

DAVE. Why not? The suicides are the best ones. *(Looking over list.)* You've got Eugene O'Neill.

KAREN. Attempted, didn't succeed.

DAVE. Cool, zoom in on this, Paulie: failed suicide, my favorite. Kinda like failing at failing, which kinda makes it succeeding, am I right?

(A pop of light. PAUL puts the camera on a tripod and joins DAVE watching TV. The volume is off. They laugh together; silence; laugh together; another quick laugh together—their laughter is totally in sync in time and duration.)

> DAVE. That is so—
> PAUL. Totally—
> DAVE. There he goes—
> PAUL. The left hand—
> DAVE. Nostrils—
> PAUL. Totally—
> DAVE. Genius.

(Laughter again. KAREN enters holding stack of papers, some books.)

KAREN. Guess what happened, my advisor had me apply for this grant, and, um, I applied ....

DAVE. That's great, K.

PAUL. Fantastic.

KAREN. *(DAVE and PAUL laugh again on cue.)* What are you guys—don't you want to turn the volume on?

DAVE/PAUL. No!

KAREN. But he's—singing.

PAUL. Exactly. Watch him strut.

DAVE. Watch the nostril flair.

PAUL. The hands—

DAVE. —is that not so weird looking, the flexing of the hands?

PAUL. People are weird looking.

DAVE. When they sing.

PAUL. Crazy.

DAVE. Genius.

PAUL. Totally.

DAVE. *(Fake announcer voice.)* Welcome to the mysterious world of the living human face—with the flexibility of a Gumby doll, it bends, it stretches, it grimaces like man's close cousin, the chimpanzee.

PAUL. Remember when we watched Tom Jones this way? Tom Jones is the best without the volume.

DAVE. We have to get you a tape of Tom Jones singing, he is totally genius free of volume.

(As they continue to watch:)

KAREN. It does look weird. Okay, really weird. Should I be filming this? I know you guys are just hanging out, but hey, Dave hanging out, maybe I should—

DAVE. Camera already on, K.
PAUL. Got it covered.
DAVE. Uhp, there it goes—left hand—
PAUL. Up and out. This is the big finish.
DAVE. Major nostril flare.
PAUL. Genius.

(DAVE and PAUL laugh together. They click the TV off and turn to KAREN.)

DAVE. So what's this grant?
KAREN. It's this little thing I applied for—I'm a finalist, but, um—
DAVE. That's fantastic.
PAUL. Good going. How much do you get?
KAREN. I'm just a finalist, I'll never get it.
DAVE. Of course you'll get it.
PAUL. She'll definitely get it.
KAREN. I'm glad you all think so.
DAVE. "Alas, alas, alas. I love a girl who has a very pretty neck, very pretty hands, a very pretty voice, very pretty wrists, a very pretty forehead, very pretty knees, but who is a coward."
PAUL. What are you—?
DAVE. Hello? That's from Breathless—Godard? The man? Did they teach you *nothing* in film school?

(A pop of light. PAUL faces us.)

PAUL. *(out)* **Photography is truth, and film is truth 24 times a second. Godard said that, something like that. See, I do remember something from, uh...** *(Cutting himself off.)* **Truth. Whose truth? Godard was the master of cutting out frames, patching things together without transitions. *Breathless*, his own**

**version of time-lapse photography. No one seems to know for sure
why he chopped the film to shit, eliminating any illusion of natu-
ralistic, flowing time in favor of herky-jerky disorientation, but he
did it, and now we revere him for it.**

*(A pop of light. PAUL joins KAREN and DAVE at dinner, filming
themselves.)*

PAUL. If this thing takes off, you know it really might, if
this thing takes off we're golden. I'll be able to make whatever I want.

KAREN. Isn't that what we're doing? Right now? Making
what you want—aren't we?

PAUL. That's right, but each leads to the next thing.

DAVE. Paul's gonna be big, K. *(Teasing.)* And I don't know
about you, but I, for one, don't mind being a stepping stone.

PAUL. The point is, I think there might be a little bit of a
buzz on me for about ten seconds; if we leap now, I bet we can get
some funding for Project Dave.

DAVE. I'm a project? I don't even have a log line yet.

KAREN. What's a log line?

DAVE. *(In movie trailer voice.)* "It could be your neighbor.
It could be your best friend. It could be you."

PAUL. "Coming this Spring to tiny art-house screens everywhere: what you don't know about the guy you thought you knew."

KAREN. That's terrible.

PAUL. Thanks.

DAVE. How about, "Dave's Brain: a nice place to visit, but
you wouldn't want to live there."

PAUL. A Brain in Pain.

DAVE. A pain in the brain.

PAUL. We have no idea what this movie is going to be
about, do we.

KAREN. Maybe it is about pain.

PAUL. Now that's entertainment.

KAREN. No, really. Pain as a normal state of being, a part of the spectrum.

PAUL. You would think that.

KAREN. What does that mean?

PAUL. The way you equate happiness with shallowness.

KAREN. No. But I think that anyone who denies a certain level of pain in life is out of touch.

PAUL. So if you're happy, you're automatically in denial? You have to work for happiness the way you have to work for everything else in life that's good. What happened to the pursuit of happiness? I believe in that. I'm a patriot, okay?

KAREN. You can't acquire happiness, Paul; some people seem to think you can just take up a hobby, like mountain biking, or if you could buy a country home and collect quilts somehow, somehow that's supposed to be happiness.

DAVE. Oh, but K, where's your *bourgeois-de-vivre*?

KAREN. Dave, you understand, don't you?

PAUL. Yes, Dave, you must understand: the way she idealizes—or should I say hagiographizes—a mental illness.

KAREN. I don't do that. Dave, do you think I do that?

DAVE. I think what K's saying, Paul, if you listen very closely to tonality and pitch and observe body language and so forth, is that she loves you very much and you should really not give her such a hard time about who she is because a lot of guys would kill for a woman like K.

KAREN. Thank you, Dave.

(A pop of light.)

KAREN. *(out)* **Do I romanticize it? Maybe. Maybe I do. This is probably going to sound pretty sick, but I think I'm kind of ... okay, jealous. Of the ones who—attempt. I mean it's not** something I would do, something I would ever consider doing in a million years, but I think in our culture we have this kind of horrible love-hate relationship with the idea of...suffering. I mean how do you get to be a saint, after all? Suffering is supposed to ennoble, and people who have suffered seem more ... worthy, somehow? Closer to God? Because somehow, suffering singles us out—makes us feel strangely chosen somehow—I don't know. This is so wrong-headed I think, but there it is. I mean Sylvia Plath and Virginia Woolf? Those women, those were my heros.

(A pop of light. KAREN and PAUL together.)

KAREN. Maybe the reason we're together is that we love each other's opposites.

PAUL. What does that mean?

KAREN. I seem weak, and yet you love my strength. You seem strong, but I love your weakness.

PAUL. I think you love me because I do understand you.

KAREN. Either that, or I love that you misunderstand me in exactly the way I want to be misunderstood.

PAUL. There's also simple chemistry. Maybe people get together because they like each other's smell; simple as that.

KAREN. That's all it is?

PAUL. Chemical.

KAREN. We need to turn the camera off so I can yell at you.

PAUL. *(Going to her; seducing.)* How about if we just keep it on.

(A pop of light. KAREN sits on the couch with her laptop and research books. DAVE on the couch, cutting and taping together pages of his novel.)

DAVE. The collage novel. It's almost all there, it's just in the wrong order.

KAREN. You know if you deigned to use a computer, there's this thing called "Cut and Paste"?

DAVE. A feature designed to drive a manic depressive crazy; I'd cut and paste myself into a dither. *(Deflecting a look between them.)* How's the Countess?

KAREN. Have you ever noticed that love and hate are both four-letter words?

DAVE. And surprisingly easy to transmogrify, one into the other: love, dove, dote, date, hate. *(Off her look.)* That's a doublet—change one letter at a time to get from one word to another, shortest path wins—

KAREN. Invented by Charles Dodgson a.k.a. Lewis Carroll, I know. I wrote a paper on him. What's your excuse?

DAVE. We bipolarly disordered, we're very fond of word games.

KAREN. *(A beat.)* We should be setting you up.

DAVE. For pratfalls?

KAREN. No, really, it isn't fair; we have to share you.

DAVE. You're right, how I going to get an adoring public if I'm never in public?

KAREN. We should—film you on dates. Outside of the house. "Open up the story," isn't that the term? I'm going to fix you up.

DAVE. Do please fix me up. Humpty Dumpty, all patched back together.

KAREN. There must be someone you've got your eye on.

DAVE. Other than my best friend's girlfriend?

KAREN. *(Re camera.)* Is this still on? How long has this been on?

(PAUL enters.)

PAUL. What have you kooky kids captured in my absence?

KAREN. You're wasting a lot of film. Leaving this on all the time.

PAUL. Tape isn't that expensive. We have to shoot everything, shape it in the editing room.

KAREN. You shouldn't leave it on without saying anything. This isn't Big Brother.

PAUL. I didn't leave it on.

DAVE. I turned it on.

KAREN. You did?

DAVE. I don't want to miss a magic moment.

(PAUL watches KAREN and DAVE exchange a look.)

PAUL. *(out)* **As the director, I get to choose the angles at which you'll witness the action. I get to decide which is more important; the mouth on the face, the hand on the cup or the window in the background. I get to tell you what to see. I get to try, anyway. My job is manipulation.** *(To KAREN and DAVE.)* You know what's been missing? A little Scotch now and then, that's what's been missing. *(Opening a bottle of Scotch and heading back with glasses.)* Who else could use a drink? I mean—sorry, Dave, I know you can't have anything. Karen?

KAREN. No, thanks.

DAVE. Go ahead, K, it doesn't bother me. Watch Karen and Paul kick back some Scotch while poor crazy Dave drinks Shirley Temples. Not to worry, I prefer to get my kicks elsewhere.

(DAVE lights up a joint.)

PAUL. You really shouldn't do that, either.

DAVE. Ah, yes, my finely tuned brain chemistry held in delicate balance ever so tenuously. Nothing wrong with a little imbalance, I say. K?

KAREN. God, it's been years. I'd—rather not.

DAVE. Oh, don't tell me you've sworn off fun, too. I live with the two most morose, morbid so-called "sane" people I've ever met.

PAUL. Hey, I'm Mr. Superficial Happiness Guy, remember? You're supposed to be the gloomy one.

DAVE. You're right. I'm doing too well. That's why you're losing interest, both of you.

KAREN. No one's losing interest.

PAUL. That's crazy.

DAVE. Not crazy enough. This movie isn't about anything unless I'm about to lose my mind.

PAUL. Why don't you talk about your suicide attempts. The Aspirin Wars, you used to call them?

DAVE. My mother is going to see this.

PAUL. You can't think about that. Don't censor yourself. Just talk. Describe what it was like.

DAVE. I'll talk about what I want to talk about.

PAUL. Then there's no point doing this.

DAVE. So turn it off.

PAUL. Full disclosure.

KAREN. He said turn it off, Paul.

PAUL. How many times? *(DAVE lunges for the camera. PAUL and DAVE struggle over control of the camera.)* I thought you wanted me to make something real. I'm getting real. You want to make this movie or not?

KAREN. *(To Paul.)* Turn it *off.*

(DAVE breaks free, holding onto the camera. He holds it for a moment. They watch him.)

DAVE. Okay, then. *(DAVE places the camera in PAUL's*

hands and puts himself in the line of focus.) Three attempts, all between the ages of twenty and twenty-five. I wanted to get someplace else. Anywhere. Nowhere. "Thousands are born so that a few may live." Remember that, Paulie? From science class—that flick about sea turtles? Scurrying across the sand to get to the ocean, most of them eaten along the way. My life a little stretch of sand. The predator in this case, my own brain. No war, famine, or crazed killers. Just myself to blame. And an ocean to get to. That I can't seem to get to. So why not?

(A pop of light as light goes out on DAVE.)

PAUL. *(out)* **Did I tell you yet that Dave was the smartest kid our class? And the thing is he wasn't just book smart, he was smart smart, he was "I think I'll just put off writing this paper till the five minute break before class and still do the best of anyone" smart. Was I jealous of Dave? Yes. Okay. Everyone was, in that way. But I loved him, you know, and I wasn't jealous of him and Karen. If I were jealous, threatened, insecure, would I have ever ....** *(To DAVE.)* You need to do me a favor, Dave.

DAVE. I'd say I owe you one or two million by now.

PAUL. I've got to prep for my shoot tomorrow; they just changed the whole script. You'll take Karen to that thing tonight?

DAVE. Paul, you have to escort your girlfriend to all galas in which she is to be the recipient of an award, that's in the good boyfriend manual.

PAUL. It's not an award. It's not. It's a grant.

DAVE. Is it a Hugh or a Carey?

PAUL. She doesn't care about this thing. Ask her, she doesn't.

DAVE. To dissemble: to conceal true feelings under a false appearance. K's very good at that, if you haven't noticed.

PAUL. I can only go by what she tells me, and she tells me she's lost all interest in the Countess and thinks the whole thing is stupid. Conclusion: she doesn't care about what she's doing, and I do care about what I'm doing and I'm willing to admit that.

DAVE. And what *are* you doing?

PAUL. You know this is my first episodic. If I don't go in and prep tonight I'm going to fuck up my break.

DAVE. I thought the donuts were your break.

PAUL. They were the break that helped me get a real break.

DAVE. What about our movie?

PAUL. Our movie, making our movie, costs money, doing outside jobs makes money.

DAVE. If we need more money, maybe I can come up with something....

PAUL. I don't want you to fund it. It's not just the money. We need credibility. Doing these jobs is giving me credibility. Now can you help me out here? They changed over half this script. Karen will be just as happy to go with you.

DAVE. *(Giving in.)* I'm supposed to be the unreliable one.

(PAUL hands the video camera to DAVE.)

PAUL . Tape it for me. Tell her I insisted you tape it so I could watch. Not for the movie, for me.

(A pop of light. DAVE sits across from KAREN. They sip champagne. DAVE films KAREN.)

KAREN. Thanks a lot for the support, Paulie. Good thing you weren't there anyway. Burn this tape. *(To DAVE.)* I babbled. I sounded like a loser. How badly did I babble?

DAVE. You were endearing.

KAREN. I was not endearing, unless "endearing" is a euphemism for pathetic. *(Re video camera.)* Turn that thing off, would you?

DAVE. I promised Paulie.

KAREN. Oh, stop covering for him. He doesn't care, do you, Paul.

DAVE. *(For the benefit of the camera.)* He cares so much that he's completely threatened.

KAREN. Threatened? By what?

DAVE. By you.

KAREN. By me? Ha.

DAVE. He's desperate to win things. You've won something first.

KAREN. A stupid little grant for my stupid little project.

DAVE. It isn't stupid.

KAREN. It isn't a big deal.

DAVE. Do you ever think anything you do, or have, or get, *is* a big deal?

KAREN. I know, I'll bet it's my part-time proofreading job that really gets him going.

DAVE. You've upset the balance, K. I know this because I'm quite well therapized, mad-as-a-hatterness notwithstanding. Unlike Paul, who has no idea that the real reason he needs me around is so there's always someone nearby doing worse than him.

KAREN. Two underachievers like us, we do make him look good, don't we.

DAVE. I love him, K. I really love the guy. He's my brother, he's like my brother. So when I see these things about him, these vanities covering insecurities, it only makes me love him more. And I wish I could make him feel all right so he wouldn't have to be such a bastard sometimes.

(Lights blink. PAUL watches.)

PAUL. *(out)* **I think I was supposed to hear all this. Obviously; they kept the camera on.**

KAREN. I love the bastard, too.

PAUL. *(out)* **The thing is ... I never got that far. I played it as far as Karen getting the ... okay, I played it for about one minute and the whole time I had on fast forward. I told Karen she looked great, sounded great, but I never actually bothered to really watch the thing. Not until later....**

KAREN. I love the way he tries so hard. And wants so much. Why does that move me, that part of him? The little boy who wants the gold stars so damn badly.

DAVE. When we were kids, he'd get pissed if someone else got chosen to lead the lunch line, even though it was alphabetical. *(KAREN laughs.)*

KAREN. We should put my grant money into our film.

DAVE. No way. The grant's for you and your Countess.

KAREN. The world's had enough of "The Beauty of the Century"; so have I, it turns out. I'd rather have more of you.

DAVE. Why did you choose her?

KAREN. My topic?

DAVE. The Countess.

KAREN. I—I don't know. I saw the photographs—the last oneS, she called it the Series of the Roses, where as an old woman she tries to recapture the beauty and glory of her youth—I was interested. In that idea. This woman who became a martyr to her own beauty by trying to idealize it even after it was gone. When I saw the photographs, I felt this connection—no, wait, that's a lie. That's not it. You see, I never found her all that beautiful. She had this whole cult following, when she was alive and even after she'd died, but I've never really been able to see it. Isn't that crazy? I'm writing about The Beauty of the Century, and I don't find her beautiful at all. Maybe— maybe it was Pierre-Louis Pierson. Her photographer. Standing at his camera, in front of this opulent background tapestry but looking more like a small, humble guy trying to serve the whims of his patron— well, it was him, I think, that drew me in. He never did manage to capture her beauty. That's what he said. He never managed to convey what those who saw her in real life must have seen. But he spent forty years trying.

DAVE. This is awful.

KAREN. I told you, so much time wasted; all I'm doing is wasting time writing about wasted time.

DAVE. No, what I'm feeling. For you. I'm in love with you, K. It's okay, don't look so worried.

KAREN. I'm not. I've got bubbles in my head. We're both drunk and stupid and we'd regret, we'd regret any ... um ... untoward—

DAVE. If you're used to regretting almost everything you do, it doesn't seem like such a big deal.

KAREN. Unaccountability. It's so appealing sometimes. It would be so nice to be completely unaccountable.

DAVE. You just have to be really young, or really old, or really crazy. But I wouldn't want you to have to live in the land of regret.

KAREN. I'm going to shut this off now.

DAVE. Shall we rewind?

KAREN. Bye, Paul.

DAVE. What if—

(KAREN turns off the camera. PAUL turns to us as lights go out on KAREN and DAVE.)

PAUL. *(out)* "What if." "What if" what? "What if" we run off together, leave poor Paulie in the dust? "What if" we're the ones meant to be together? "What if" Paulie changes, promises to change? "What if" we make love just once, and never tell the sap, because after all he's the one who set this whole thing up, he deserves it, doesn't he?

KAREN. I'm going to shut this off now.

DAVE. Shall we rewind?

KAREN. Bye, Paul.

DAVE. What if—

PAUL. *(out)* **What if what I need, what I'm looking for, the thing that will make it all make sense somehow, is just outside the frame—somewhere in between or beyond or—**

(A pop of light. PAUL enters the scene.)

PAUL. You—you drank with him?

KAREN. I— to celebrate, yes....

DAVE. That is what one does with champagne. Of course one can also bathe in it.

PAUL. All your research, and you let him get drunk?

DAVE. "Let" him?

KAREN. And we didn't get drunk.

PAUL. You know he has a really delicate balance.

KAREN. We hardly—what did we have, a glass I guess— I guess I didn't think.

DAVE. Hello. K is not my caretaker. Besides, I wasn't mixing anything with my medication. So don't blame K, okay? *(A slight pause.)* See the thing is, I stopped taking my pills.

PAUL. *(Quietly.)* What?

DAVE. I did it for my doc.

PAUL. Your doctor approved?

DAVE. My doc—umentary. Don't you want to capture me in all my wondrous states of being?

PAUL. *(After a beat.)* How long ago did you stop?

DAVE. I want you to see the real me. Show people who I really am. Not the medicated, propped-up, suitable for polite society version.

PAUL. If you haven't figured out what a bad idea not taking your pills is by now.

DAVE. I can handle it. You guys are right here if anything goes wrong.

PAUL. That's insane.

DAVE. And I'm insane. How can we make an honest movie if I can't be my honest self?

KAREN. But isn't it dishonest to do something that you wouldn't normally do, just for the movie?

PAUL. He didn't do it for the movie. The movie is a fucking excuse.

DAVE. I'm an Arctic explorer leading the way to the topmost and the bottom-most and you don't know, you have no idea what an amazing view you can get from way up on the North Pole.

PAUL. Would it be so bad to settle for normal?

DAVE. Yes, it would. And this is my normal, as it happens. This is me, the real me, not the drugged-up trying-to-pass-like-everyone-else fake me. I don't want to take pills for the rest of my life.

PAUL. You're fucking lucky they've got them.

DAVE. What would you do if someone said they'd take away your pain, easy-peasy, oh, but there's one little condition here, better check the fine print: no pain, but no joy, either. Would you accept those terms?

PAUL. Mania is not joy.

DAVE. You need to think that. Zombies want to turn everyone else into zombies. But you don't know, you have no idea, how amazing life can be when everything glows and it flows and it shines with meaning and purpose and soul.

PAUL. You want me to save you, Dave? Or is that "K"'s job now?

DAVE. I do not need to be saved. I save. I am the savior here. I am saving your movie, your whole career, Big Director Man. You need me now and you don't like that you need me.

(A pop of light. PAUL faces us.)

PAUL. *(out)* **A movie is a series of still images. Action broken down to its smallest separate—components. Motion, like time, is an optical illusion.**

(A pop of light. Late at night. DAVE is writing furiously on the couch.)

DAVE. I'm on a roll, guys. I feel like I must practically glow, man. Is anyone filming this? HELLO! WAKE UP, TROOPS! GOOD MORNING, VIETNAM! DOESN'T ANYONE WANT TO CATCH THIS ACT? This is the climax! This is the dénouement!

(PAUL enters with the camera.)

PAUL. What are you doing?

DAVE. I'm finishing my novel. I'm in the Zone, Paulie. OH KA-AY! RISE AND SHINE, WE NEED YOU IN THE WAR ROOM! James Joyce took, what, like thirteen years to write Ulysses? And I've been working, what, a year, and I don't know, Paulie, I shouldn't say anything yet, but I really think this is better.

PAUL. Have you slept at all?

DAVE. Sleep is for wooses. I'm going to give you the film rights, Paulie. GET YOUR BUTT OUT HERE, K!

(KAREN enters just behind PAUL, just awakened.)

KAREN. What time is it?

DAVE. *(Rapid fire.)* You and K, you're gonna make the movie version. And I think it's too good to be a movie, I mean it's too complex, but Henry James works on film and I think if anyone can capture it, I think you guys can. I mean hey, The Idiot, right, K?

KAREN. Why don't you read us what you've got?

DAVE. I need this on film, Paul. What, are you afraid I'm writing "All work and no play makes Dave a dull boy" a hundred times over? Trust me, it's brilliant.

KAREN. Read some.

DAVE. I don't know if I'm ready to blow your mind. Everywhere you look, there's poetry, there's magic, poof, bunny from the hat, mad hatter, hat on a bunny, turn on the camera and call action and catch the action I am in. Is this not brilliance? As in shine, as in sparkle, as in see yourself in reflected glory that's the story, is it not?

KAREN. Are you okay?

DAVE. "Okay"? I'm better than okay. I'm bursting, K. The world, the world is full of music but it's in your head and you have to listen at night because during the day the sounds will drown you out, people drown, more children drown in swimming pools than by gunfire did you know that? But then why should any child die by gunfire that's what I say, one is too many that's what I say, people need to swim more, turn off that fucking camera, will you?

PAUL. You woke me up to turn it on.

DAVE. Soul sapper. That's what that machine is. Sacrilege— that's what's going on here. Creating images as if you are God, creating false gods, you are not God.

(PAUL keeps the camera on DAVE.)

DAVE. Turn that off. Turn that off, the second commandment commands you not, no graven images no images in the image of God and I am that image I am a divine being turn that off, you call yourself a Jew, you, you hypocrite. St. David, that's who I am, a martyr to your sins and this is my feast day, my fucking feast day, and I was thinking about the movie and the movie is the future, the movie is my past when I am in the future and no one's thinking about the future because it comes too fast, it's always on the way and before you know it it's tomorrow and tomorrow and tomorrow creeping in its petty pace but I don't think it's so petty as it turns out, I think it's fucking fast and furious and it doesn't creep, it careens, it cruises, it crashes into Schiller and Schelling and Schopenhauer and sud- denly—

KAREN. *(Overlapping.)* I'll call his doctor. The hospital. Who should I call? *(PAUL zooms the camera in on DAVE.)*

DAVE. —suddenly it becomes clear that they didn't live before us, they live after us on a loop, an infinite loop and all our yes- terdays have lighted fools the way to dusty death and all our tomor- rows cast a long dark shadow over our todays, that's what I think, Mr. William Shakespeare, if you catch my drift.

(Pop of light. PAUL faces us.)

PAUL. *(out)* **Rapid cycling—when the time between epi- sodes keeps getting shorter. Like a negative, where everything dark becomes light. And everything light becomes dark. And ... and this should probably be a dissolve.**

(DAVE curls up on couch.)

DAVE. God hates me. For some reason God hates me. Why else would he make my brain like this? Why does God hate me, Paulie?

(A pop of light. PAUL steps forward.)

PAUL. *(out)* **I survive. I come from a long line of The Ones Who Got Out, so ... maybe that makes us—hearty? Re- sourceful? Lucky? Is there a gene for that—luck? Or is it that we were the ruthless ones, the ambitious ones, the self-preserving devious disingenuous motherfuckers of the lot. I survive, which makes it my job, don't you think, to be the designated Witness?**

To record what I can? Isn't that what survivors do? I pick up the camera. I aim. I shoot.

(PAUL turns his camera onto DAVE.)

      PAUL. *(To DAVE.)* Talk to me. Go on Dave. What you're feeling.

      KAREN. Dave? Dave, you're okay. You'll be okay. Say something, Dave.

(No pop of light as the scene shifts and Paul backs away. DAVE gets into a hospital bed. KAREN sits beside him holding a box of chocolates. She bites into a piece.)

      KAREN. This chocolate is like so amazing, you have to try it. *(Off DAVE's silence)* There's got to be a pleasure, a simple pleasure that you can appreciate ... that you can say shit, I've got to get better, I've got to see sand dunes and listen to Mozart and taste chocolate.

      DAVE. Insipid, K.

      KAREN. I know, but it's really, really great chocolate. *(Beat)* You'll get through this. We will. We'll get you through. I want you to get well. Please get well.

(KAREN kisses DAVE.)

      DAVE. Mercy kiss? Okay if it was. I'll take it anyway.

(A pop of light. PAUL turns to KAREN.)

      PAUL. Why are you telling me this?

      KAREN. I want you to know. And I didn't kiss him out of pity, if that's what you mean.

PAUL. I didn't say pity. Compassion. A compassion kiss. I can live with that.

KAREN. I kissed him because I wanted to and I fucking enjoyed it.

PAUL. So you're leaving me for Dave?

KAREN. Not "for" Dave. No.

PAUL. "Because" of him, then.

KAREN. We need time apart.

PAUL. We haven't even had time together.

KAREN. *(Picking up camera to film.)* Plenty of time, Paul.

PAUL. Time with no one in between. Can you put down the camera?

KAREN. "Honest film." "Full disclosure." Maybe we needed an in-between.

PAUL. *(Waving away camera.)* Karen, please.

KAREN. "You're part of the story now."

PAUL. Can we please talk to each other here?

KAREN. We are talking. Ignore me. Ignore this.

PAUL. The movie was your idea.

KAREN. You're right. It was. And I'm trying to tell you, I don't know what's real anymore. What's "true." And I'm not going to figure it out if I stay.

PAUL. You can turn off the fucking camera.

KAREN. The camera stays. I go.

(KAREN hands PAUL the camera.)

PAUL. I don't know how to do this scene with any originality, but I'm lost without you.

KAREN. *(A moment's hesitation.)* You only think that when I'm halfway out the door.

PAUL. We can make this work. Why are you doing this?

KAREN. *(Facing camera.)* I always wanted to be one of

those what-the-hell girls ...

(A pop of light.)

      KAREN. ... but I'm not.

(KAREN goes. PAUL takes a deep breath, downs his Scotch and Xanax.)

      PAUL. *(out)* **When you're deeply involved in a game of push-me pull-you, the best thing you can do to win someone over is to get over them. I took a couple of Dave's old Xanax and sat with a glass of Scotch. I am fully capable of pretending to move on.** *(To DAVE.)* Your own place; this is fantastic.

      DAVE. Karen found it for me.

      PAUL. I know, Dave. I'm well aware. *(out)* **She helped him move in to the apartment below the one she'd found for herself. She even gave him our couch. I was couchless for months. But I thought Dave setting up his own life right near Karen, whom I knew I would win back with my intermittent bouts of indifference and passion, was a good thing for everyone.** *(To DAVE.)* I think this is a real step forward.

      DAVE. Who's Ward?

      PAUL. What?

      DAVE. A step for-ward. But is it a step for Ward or a step for Dave?

      PAUL. That's really dumb, Dave.

      DAVE. Or is it a step back to-ward the psycho ward?

      PAUL. Puns, the lowest form of humor.

      DAVE. So said some humorless non-punner. How many puns does it take to screw in a light bulb?

      PAUL. I don't know.

      DAVE. Two, but they usually prefer to screw in a place

where there's at least a divan or a shag carpet and a fireplace and stuff. You laughed. I heard you laugh.

      PAUL. I did not laugh.
      DAVE. Internally.

(PAUL picks up a stack of pages.)

      PAUL. You're working.
      DAVE. I'm going to finish the novel for real this time. The movie can't end with my still not having finished it, you know?

(PAUL picks up the camera to film DAVE.)

      PAUL. Read some of what you've got?
      DAVE. Not yet, Paulie. I wish I could have been an engineer, a guy inventing bridges. That is such a profound thing to do with your life.
      PAUL. Okay. But finishing your novel's not a bad thing to do, either.
      DAVE. I've been writing all these separate pieces and I need to link them up so I started reading about bridges and bridges, when you think about bridges, you suddenly understand how everything connects to every other thing. That's what we should do, make a documentary about bridges. Is it too late to change our topic here?
      PAUL. You're joking, right? We've got footage.
      DAVE. We can connect the footage to my headage through discussion of the bipolar brain bridge.
      PAUL. I'm not making a documentary about bridges, Dave.
      DAVE. Bridges that have broken. *(Grabbing a book.)* Listen to this, this is, like, the most breathtaking shit: "The function of a bridge is the continuation of a roadway over a void... its structure is both means and end ... its reality lies not in the space enclosed, as in a building, but in the space itself."

(KAREN enters as PAUL recedes, watching.)

KAREN. Bridges. That is such a cool idea.

DAVE. You think so?

KAREN. I love that idea. And, and in a way, you know, Pierson's camera, that was a bridge that allowed him to connect to society—to the Countess—past to future, present to past, camera as bridge— wow, I'm getting excited about my subject again. But it's your idea.

DAVE. Newsflash, K, bridges are not my idea. Ideas are in the atmosphere, they belong to everyone who breathes.

KAREN. I can't wait to read your novel.

DAVE. You'll be the first.

KAREN. Can I read what you've got?

DAVE. *(Suddenly turning on her.)* Will you stop asking me that?

KAREN. What?

DAVE. You're always asking me that. You're so in my face sometimes. Have you ever thought about the fact that you're kind of a smothering personality?

KAREN. I—

DAVE. Really, I would just like you to leave me alone for ten seconds, okay? Silence is not a bad thing. Okay? Just because two people are together doesn't mean they have to talk all the time. Have you thought about the fact that I might really need to have some *silence* in order to *think*? I'm sorry, but my thoughts are loud, okay?

(A pop of light. KAREN and PAUL.)

KAREN. Do I romanticize it? Maybe. Maybe I do.

PAUL. It wasn't you, Karen. It was … the disease. Help me finish it?

KAREN. I can't. *(Starts to go; turns back.)* You know there's this one picture—it's the most famous, the one where the Countess holds a black frame to her eye and looks back at us. She called it Scherzo di Follia. A game of folly. Maybe she knew that's what all of it was -- attempting to capture the past, to preserve it for the future— thinking you can change the sequence of time—isn't that in itself a madness?

(A pop of light. DAVE's apartment; PAUL is showing him scenes from the movie on the computer.)

DAVE. *(Voiceover.)* —suddenly it becomes clear that they didn't live before us, they live after us on a loop, an infinite loop and all our yesterdays have lighted fools the way to dusty death and all our tomorrows cast a long dark shadow over our todays, that's what I think, Mr. William Shakespeare, if you catch my drift.

DAVE. I'm crazy. Look at me, I'm fucking crazy.

PAUL. This is why an actor should never watch his own dailies.

DAVE. I wasn't acting. I was drooling.

PAUL. It wasn't your best look, I admit.

DAVE. Jesus. Do I always drool when I'm in that state?

PAUL. You wanted to see what we've got so far.

DAVE. Well I didn't know I drooled. Has K seen this? Or— K's okay, right?

PAUL. You'd know better than me.

DAVE. You guys belong together. The Countess and the Filmographer. And introducing the third wheel … The Drooler.

PAUL. You're fine. It's the movie I'm not so sure about. All this footage, but where does it go. I need to find a shape.

DAVE. Maybe I have no shape. What we need is a hook. Or is it a noose? How would you like to film that?

PAUL. I wouldn't.

DAVE. But would you?

PAUL. What?

DAVE. You don't have the balls, do you.

PAUL. What are you talking about?

DAVE. To make this movie.

PAUL. I'm making it—

DAVE. The movie sucks.

PAUL. Thank you, Dave, very supportive.

DAVE. The movie sucks. And the movie is all I've got. If I slashed my wrists right here, right now, do you have the cajones to see it through? Well? Do you have what it takes or not?

PAUL. Dave, please—I can't do this right now.

DAVE. Admit it. Admit you botched it.

PAUL. Go to hell.

DAVE. It's not your fault. It's me. I'm back on the couch. I'm back on the fucking couch. I don't think I'm going to make it off the couch, Paulie, and you have to admit there's not much of a movie in that.

PAUL. The movies is going to be fine. And so are you. You're doing really well.

DAVE. Too bad it's when I'm *not* well that I occasionally get to feel—myself. That I see connections and am right in my skin and for once I'm not full of despair, and shame, and anger, and no hope. Too bad when I'm not well I feel the stars we're made of and I get a taste of how life can be better than it always, otherwise, is.

PAUL. Everything's a trade-off.

DAVE. Fuck you and your "trade offs."

PAUL. Are you taking your medication?

DAVE. I'm taking the lithium, okay. I'm taking the lithium and the trithium and the zinithium and the depecoate and the winter coat and Dr. V's adding paprika and oregano and a little basil 'cause the salt just ain't cutting it anymore, but I don't think anyone'll be happy until I'm smothered in A-1 sauce.

PAUL. You'll see your doctor tomorrow. We'll find something better for you to take.

DAVE. Recalibrated every few months when I get dry mouth or gain weight or can't stop twirling my tongue or shaking my hands or *drooling* and that's on the normal days but maybe there's a medication to counter the medication and when that stops working there's always another medication and I think I have a right to decide whether or not I want to live this way.

PAUL. You're not going off your meds. I can't go through that with you again.

DAVE. Not asking you to. All I am asking for is the final reel. Or is it my unreel. My real reel.

PAUL. I should go.

DAVE. That's right. You should go ahead. Go on. We tried. You gave it your best shot, Paulie. We both did.

PAUL. What do you want from me?

DAVE. I need your help, Paulie. I can't keep trekking back and forth to hell on earth like this. My visa's expired, worn out from over-use, no more extensions, Dude.

PAUL. We'll go to the hospital.

DAVE. Leave the camera for me, Paulie. Leave it on a tripod and let me decide this one thing, one thing in my life.

PAUL. You—this is not you talking.

DAVE. Not little voices speaking in my head yet, thanks. But you're right: how do I know when my brain's going to decide to betray me, take a little expedition, hurt the people I love? How can anybody trust me, how can I trust me? So I throw in the towel. So I do that now instead of dragging it out ten, twenty, thirty, God help me fifty more years of this. I need this movie to have an end, Paulie. I need an end.

PAUL. You don't end. You, you write. You take your medicine. You get happy. You get a dog. You fall in love. Not necessarily in that particular order. You struggle like the rest of us.

DAVE. No, see, I don't "struggle like the rest of us." I'm sick. I've always been sick. I'm sick to death of being sick.

PAUL. We finish the movie. We do a promotional tie-in with your brilliant novel. You sign copies to groupies.

DAVE. It's not happening, Paulie. It's never going to happen. *(DAVE pours out a garbage pail-full of shredded paper.)* Said novel. Dread novel. Dead novel.

(PAUL picks up some of the shredded paper.)

PAUL. Why?

DAVE. I started to reread it and I think it was pretty bad, Paulie. I think it was embarrassingly bad. I wanted to make something beautiful and it wasn't.

PAUL. You can't judge your own work.

DAVE. It's okay, Paulie, I don't need it anymore. I have the movie now. Self-expression. Thanks to you, I am expressed. You'll get it right eventually. I'm counting on you. *(Turning camera on himself.)* Am I an action-adventure, a romantic comedy? I know: a horror flick. A freak show. A slasher thriller.

PAUL. Please stop.

DAVE. If you give me a way out, and a way to not feel so alone on my way out, I think I might be able to stay in.

PAUL. What do you want? My blessing?

DAVE. Yes.

PAUL. I can't.

DAVE. Leave the camera for me and give me one night's peace of mind. I know you understand, Paulie. You're the only one who does.

PAUL. *(out)* **A long time ago I made a promise. It was simple, and I didn't know what it meant at the time.**

(DAVE stays in the background, on the couch.)

DAVE. Don't leave me behind, Paulie.

PAUL. *(out)* **Dave was my best friend from the time we were little, our memories are filled with each other, our whole—**

DAVE. Don't leave me to the goddamn werewolves. Don't let me die a sorry-ass bum in a stinkin' motel room.

PAUL. *(out)* **Our whole lives.**

DAVE. I'm not joking, Paulie. You gotta keep me off the ratty couch. Promise. Promise me.

PAUL. *(Becoming the younger self.)* Whatever, Hummer.

DAVE. You gotta promise me.

PAUL. I promise. God. Whatever.

(PAUL shakes off the memory and finishes rigging the tripod for DAVE. He comes forward, leaving him on the couch.)

PAUL. *(out)* **The film transfer was the most expensive element. I edited it the old-fashioned way with film, spools of film, and, ah—**

(DAVE sits, lit in a separate space. He leans forward and adjusts the camera.)

DAVE. "The Tacoma Narrows Bridge was ruptured by wind and collapsed four months after its completion in 1940. It had a twenty-eight hundred foot span. It had weight, gravity, and pressure, while at the same time evoking ... flight. A single splendid gesture dedicated to the conquest of space. Was it less beautiful to behold for proving unable to withstand the forces of nature?" Beginning of said novel. Or the end. Fragment.

PAUL. *(out)* **In film school they teach you that an audience will forgive you almost anything at the beginning of a movie, but almost nothing at the end. They're counting on the fact that we have short memories. In life it's the reverse, I think. We learn**

to forgive more as we go on. At least ... that's what I'm hoping.
DAVE. Anyway I think it's only fair that I get the last word, don't you? Try not to append. *(Clicks on a CD. It should be the same song we heard at the beginning, something they listened to in high school, with a Steely Dan beat.)* See, I'm looking out for you, Paulie. I've even got the soundtrack. K, don't let him go the Janice, Jimmi, Cobain route in any case. *(Adjusting camera.)* Dave alone. Alone with the camera. If a tree falls in the forest and no one is watching but a satellite dish captures the event for the CIA to see .... That's a joke. No paranoia at present. Alone with a camera. To do with as I wish. To see what I am when I am alone. Who I am. And who I am not. Who I intend not to be. To be not. *(Lining up his pill bottles.)* Jump. Cut. To jump or to cut, which shall it be? Let us go gently .... *(Swallows a pill.)* Where do we go next? Someplace unexpected would be nice. Jump cut to somewhere else, anywhere else.... *(Swallows another pill.)* You may wonder: am I thinking clearly? Yes, for once. In my right mind. Which, unfortunately, happens to be a wrong mind. For this world anyway. I've worn out my welcome, and I won't get better. Or if I do, I'll only get worse again after, which makes the whole getting-better phase so much more difficult to enjoy. Clarity for once. Clarity and peace. Saturn is so close, so close at hand, so bright and perfect and God is ready for me—or should I say: And I am ready for God. And I am tired. And I just need, so badly, to sleep.

(DAVE swallows a handful of pills. Another handful. He curls up on the couch.
The sound of a projector whirring for another moment as the lights continue to flicker. PAUL tries to face us....)

PAUL. *(out)* I ... I ...I don't know where to begin...

(...he can't. The word "begin" floats for a moment. Blackout.)

END OF PLAY

PROPERTIES

ACT I	**Set Dressing/Trim Props**	**Actor Props**
Scenes:		
Apartment	Sofa Rug Television on small enclosed stand End table with drawer Swivel office chair Stereo components: early 80's Large speakers, turntable, and amp Stacks of albums	Steely Dan's album "Any World" Bong with legal week Matches or lighter
Café	Café table and 2 or 3 (SLC)	Thick book: *The Lives of* *Saints* Notepad Pen or pencil
Apartment	Same as previous apartment scene	Joint Matches or lighter
Café	Same as previous café scene	Dostoevsky's *The Idiot* (paperback version) Notepad or notebook Pencil or pen Paper grocery bag with 24 cans of baking powder tins
Transition	"Dave's World"	Telephone Bottle of pills

Apartment **Kitchen Area**	Table settings for 3: silverware, plates, salad bowls, glasses, etc.	Dinner food/salad
Apartment **Living Room** **Area**		Remote control Bag of Chips Snack for Dave Video camera

ACT II *Scenes:*	**Set Dressing/Trim Props**	**Actor Props**
Apartment	Kitchen area with table and chairs *or* living area as in ACT I	Bowl of cereal and spoon Coffeemaker Cup of coffee Printouts with lists of artists, writers and composers Book 2 notepads 2 pens Bottle of Scotch 2 glasses Joint Matches or lighter
	Books Stacks of paper	Video camera Picture of a woman in a black frame Donuts Bottle of champagne 2 champagne glasses Bottle of pills

		Many boxes of different teas Many mugs Teach kettle and teapot Sugar and creamer
Hospital Room	Appropriate set dressing	Box of chocolates (2 eaten each performance) Humor books (paperback) Coffee mugs Other small humorous gifts
Apartment	Same as previous scenes	Stack of pages from Dave's notebook Book about bridges
Editing Room	Appropriate set dressing	Scissors (break apart) Paper for cutting shapes Garbage pail full of shredded paper CD player/Steely Dan Pill bottles
Transition	"Paul's World"	16mm projector Film canister

Searing Satires
from
Thomas Bradshaw

PURITY
(#17853)

A refined and prominent African-American English professor's life is turned upside down when a new, 'more black' professor is hired in his department and challenges his authenticity, his marriage to a white woman, and his entire way of life. This way of life consists of literature, booze, cocaine binges, and pedophilia. From realism to fantasy, Purity takes us on a journey from the Ivy League to the ante-bellum South to the fields of Ecuador and back again, ending on a note of shocking violence.

PROPHET
(#18714)

A man wakes up one morning and decides he must kill himself. He is angry with himself for not hitting his wife every time she has an independent thought (as Abraham and Moses would have done). After she dies and God reveals to him that he is the new Prophet, the man takes a new wife, dresses her in slave chains, and begins to preach his newfound gospel of male domination. Simultaneously humorous and disturbing, Bradshaw's Prophet explores controversial issues in startling and unexpected ways.

The Clean House
By Sarah Ruhl
2005 Pulitzer Prize Finalist

This extraordinary new play by an exciting new voice in the American drama was runner-up for the Pulitzer Prize. The play takes place in what the author describes as "metaphysical Connecticut", mostly in the home of a married couple who are both doctors. They have hired a housekeeper named Matilde, an aspiring comedian from Brazil who's more interested in coming up with the perfect joke than in house-cleaning. Lane, the lady of the house, has an eccentric sister named Virginia who's just nuts about house-cleaning. She and Matilde become fast friends, and Virginia takes over the cleaning while Matilde works on her jokes. Trouble comes when Lane's husband Charles reveals that he has found his soul mate, or "bashert" in a cancer patient named Anna, on whom he has operated. The actors who play Charles and Anna also play Matilde's parents in a series of dream-like memories, as we learn the story about how they literally killed each other with laughter, giving new meaning to the phrase, "I almost died laughing." This theatrical and wildly funny play is a whimsical and poignant look at class, comedy and the true nature of love. 1m, 4f (#6266)

"Fresh, funny ... a memorable play, imbued with a somehow comforting philosophy: that the messes and disappointments of life are as much a part of its beauty as romantic love and chocolate ice cream, and a perfect punch line can be as sublime as the most wrenchingly lovely aria." — *NY Times*

THE BASIC CATALOGUE OF PLAYS AND MUSICALS
online at samuelfrench.com